FRASER

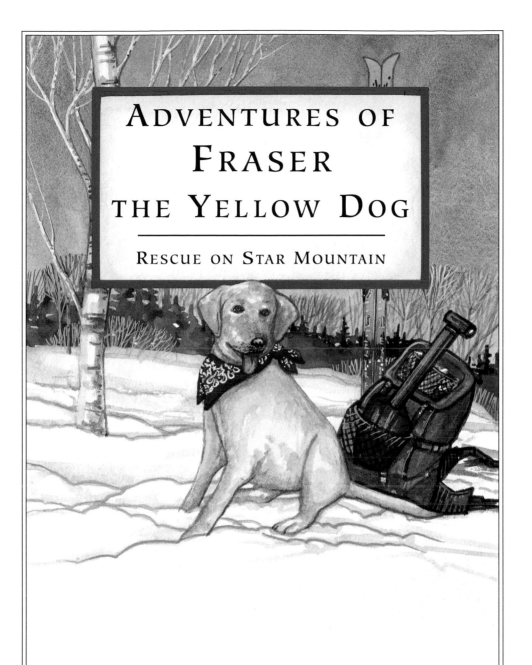

ADVENTURES OF
FRASER
THE YELLOW DOG

RESCUE ON STAR MOUNTAIN

BY JILL SHEELEY

ILLUSTRATED BY TAMMIE LANE

COURTNEY PRESS

First edition published in 1999 by Courtney Press, Aspen, Colorado
Copyright © 1999 by Jill Sheeley

A very special thanks to Rob Seideman, Tammie Lane, my family and all my many friends who gave me advice and support.

This is a fictional story. The girls ski "alone" to the mountain cabin in this story for the sake of adventure, but in real life, the author recommends skiing with adult supervision!

Library of Congress Catalog Card Number: 99-96059

For information about ordering this book, write: Jill Sheeley • P.O. Box 845 • Aspen, CO 81612 or email aac@rof.net

Printed in Korea.
ISBN 0-9609108 6-7

I'd like to dedicate this book to all the many volunteers in towns all across the country who devote their time, energy and love to saving dogs. Check into your local humane society. Dogs are friends for life!

A very special thanks to the Scandinavian Design shop in Aspen, Colorado, for allowing us the opportunity to feature their gorgeous ski sweaters throughout this book.

Special thanks to the Iams Co. for making high quality, nutritious foods for Fraser and millions of other dogs around the world.

Partial proceeds from this book will be donated to P.A.W.S. (Aspen/Pitkin County Animal Shelter) and to the Eagle Valley Humane Society.

Both of these organizations facilitate the adoption of healthy, spayed and neutered dogs and cats.

May every animal be loved and cared for in a humane way - may all animals be a part of a loving family.

Courtney could not sleep. She had been preparing for tomorrow's cross-country ski trip for weeks, and now lay wrapped in her fluffy down comforter, warm as fresh bread in a basket, watching her dog, Fraser, asleep by her side.

"Just think, Fraser," she said, "you don't have to stay at home, like when I leave to go downhill skiing. You get to come with us. You get to run and play!" Fraser's ears perked; his tail wagged!

It all began in January when Courtney's mom and dad invited Courtney and her friends to cross-country ski to their mountain cabin for two days.

"Alone," Courtney announced to Katy and Taylor. "We get to ski by ourselves. My parents are going up three days earlier than us. All they asked is that we have to pack our backpacks, plus we have to *whip ourselves into shape.*"

"As if that won't be any fun," laughed Taylor.

"After our school hut trip last year," said Katy, "I've been dying to go again."

"Me too," said Taylor. "It was the coolest."

"Aren't you worried about snow slides?" Katy asked Courtney. "Like the one you were in last year?"

"No problem," said Courtney, "we don't cross any slopes steep enough to slide. My dad was on Mountain Rescue. He taught avalanche workshops. If he thought there was going to be a problem, he'd have let us know."

The girls spent the next few weeks getting ready: working out...

Playing hockey...

"Wow," said Katy. "There sure is a lot of stuff to take on a ski trip."

"First-aid gear?" said Katy.

"Check." "Space blanket?" "Check." "Headlamps?" "Check." "Shovel?" "Check." "Homemade chocolate-chip cookies?"

"That's not on the list," said Courtney.

"It is now. Lots of layers of warm clothes and a good waterproof jacket," Katy said.

"At least we don't have to bring sleeping bags," exclaimed Taylor. "That is so awesome."

"Actually, we do," said Courtney, "just in case."

Morning arrived, and Courtney met the girls at the trailhead.

"It's as cold as Fraser's nose," Courtney announced.

"No standing around, or we'll freeze," said Taylor. "Let's go."

"Just remember," Courtney reminded the group, "Number one rule in the back country is we all stay together."

The conditions were perfect, and the girls found a nice rhythm. Fraser found a rhythm of his own, leaping through the deep snow, catching powder on his muzzle as if it were a shovel. The girls sang their favorite songs for a while, but soon many of the words turned to loud, deep breaths.

"Let's stop," said Katy, "at least for a few minutes. I'm pooped."

"I'm hot," said Taylor.

"I'm hungry," said Courtney. "How about those chocolate-chip cookies? We're going to need to eat and drink a lot to keep our energy up. Fraser, too: I brought his favorite treat... dog bones."

A deer bounded out of some brush, and an ermine slipped quickly from one bush to another.

"Oh, how cute!" exclaimed Taylor. "I had to do a report on that little guy. Did you know ermines change their color to brown in the summer?"

Courtney nodded and asked, "Did you know that wild animals don't get snow clumped up in their paws, like Fraser does?"

By now the sun had made it up over the ridgeline of the surrounding mountains, and the air had warmed. The girls were cheerful. They found a gentle slope to climb, and, on the way down, practiced the telltale sign of a back-country skier: the telemark turn.

They climbed the hill again, and skied down. Then again. And again.

Finally exhausted, Courtney let herself fall backwards into a patch of tracked-up powder. What she saw was alarming: black clouds, thick and getting thicker by the second. She sat up.

"We've got to go," she warned the girls.

Without a word, Courtney, Katy and Taylor gathered up their packs and hit the trail. A frigid wind blew fiercely. The skiing wasn't so easy anymore, not with the wind pushing Courtney backwards, the freezing snow blowing in her face.

The clouds were completely socked in. Swirling snow swarmed like angry bees around Courtney's head. She turned to check on her friends. Courtney couldn't see five feet in any direction.

"We're in trouble," yelled Courtney to Katy and Taylor. "I think we should build a snow shelter. My dad taught me how."

"We'd better get to work," said Katy.

"I'm so glad Fraser's with us," Taylor finally spoke up. "He's so warm."

"This isn't so bad," laughed Katy. "We're snug as bugs in a rug."

The girls settled down. They thought of word games to play. They ate chocolate-chip cookies. They drank Gatorade®. Fraser reaped most of the attention, though, because he was the warmest.

Then suddenly, Fraser yelped, and darted out of the shelter.

Startled, Taylor asked, "I wonder where he's going?"

"Do you think there could be wolves out there?" asked Katy.

"Do you think someone's looking for us? I think I hear a snowmobile," said Courtney.

"Listen," shouted Taylor, "it's getting louder."

The girls peeked out of their shelter. Courtney recognized two Mountain Rescue workers, friends of her dad.

"Thank you so much for finding us," Courtney said to Craig and Laura. "I don't know how you did it though. We couldn't see a thing."

"Your mom and dad radioed that you hadn't arrived at the cabin on time. But you're right: without your dog, we might have skied right by you. The visibility is terrible. You girls did the right thing by staying together."

Courtney turned to Fraser, "I love you, Fraser. I don't know what we would have done without you."

"You're only a mile from the cabin," said Laura. "How about if we give you a tow?"

"Boy, are we ever glad to see you," said Courtney's mom. She had a huge grin, but Courtney could see that her mom had been scared. Her eyes looked as if she'd been crying. Courtney's dad hugged Craig.

"I can't thank you enough," said Courtney's dad, "for getting the girls home safe and sound."

"It was our pleasure," said Craig. "Fraser was the real reason we were able to find the girls. He's one smart dog."

Courtney hugged Fraser, "You'll come with us on our next adventure, won't you, boy?"

Mountain Awareness

The mountains offer us wonderful adventures. Be prepared for winter's challenges: weather changes, cold, and avalanches. Following are a few things to know when going into the back country:

- ◆ Get adjusted to the altitude before going on an adventure

- ◆ Drink plenty of water

- ◆ Eat high energy snacks — stay nourished

- ◆ Bring a first-aid kit, emergency gear, a good topographical map, and a compass

- ◆ Take an avalanche training class

- ◆ Call your local avalanche and weather forecast center before leaving on an adventure

- ◆ Know how to self-rescue in an emergency. Don't rely on cell phones or radios

- ◆ Make sure your group has leadership, route-finding and first-aid skills

- ◆ Stay with your group

Ski safely
and
have fun!